NOT QUITE PLANETS

by Glenn Taylor
Illustrated by Nathan Y. Jarvis

Published by Capstone Press, Inc.

Distributed By
CHILDRENS PRESS®
CHICAGO

CIP

LIBRARY OF CONGRESS CATALOGING IN PUBLICATION DATA

Taylor, Glenn
Not quite planets / by Glenn Taylor
Summary: Captain Contraption explains to his young traveling companions on his spaceship about asteroids, meteors, meteorites, and comets.

ISBN 1-56065-012-5

1.Asteroids--Juvenile literature. 2. Comets--Juvenile literature. 3. Meteors--Juvenile literature. [1. Asteroids. 2. Comets. 3. Meteors.]
I. Title II. Series.
QB651.T39 1989
523.4'4--dc20 **89-25196 CIP AC**

Designed by Nathan Y. Jarvis & Associates, Inc.

Capstone Press

Box 669, Mankato, MN, U.S.A. 56001

CONTENTS

WHAT COULD BE SIMPLER?

CAPTAIN CONTRAPTION picked himself up off the dark ground of the tiny **asteroid**. Broken pieces of his latest invention tumbled down in slow motion. They looked like confetti at a parade. The Captain smiled at his helpers, Cathy and Danny. A twisted piece of metal floated onto his head and slid off. In the asteroid's low **gravity**, it took more than a minute to reach the ground. "Perfect," he said. "This has all been planned."

Cathy and Danny stood in their spacesuits behind the Captain's spaceship. A few minutes earlier the Captain had fired off his latest invention. It had been a huge upside-down rocket engine aimed at the ground. At first, the rocket had sent a great orange flare hundreds of feet into the coal black sky. Then the rocket engine had started to shake apart. Finally, a huge explosion had torn it to bits. Pieces flew in all directions.

Some went out into space. Some would slowly come back to the asteroid hours later. Cathy frowned at the Captain.

"What did it do?" she asked.

"It blew up," said Danny. "That's what it did. All that work and it just blew up."

"Ha!" shouted the Captain. "That shows how much you two know. Everything you know comes from a book. But I build things!"

"We helped build that thing," Cathy reminded him. "And you don't know everything, Captain Contraption. Besides, books are a good place to start."

"You're right, of course," said the Captain. "I just hate it when people criticize me without knowing what I'm trying to do. That's all. Now, let's get back to work."

"But you still haven't told us what you're trying to do!" exclaimed Danny.

The Captain stopped and looked over at Danny. "I'm not exactly sure yet. My upside-down rocket was supposed to push the asteroid out of the **asteroid belt**!"

The three of them leaped gently and gracefully over the sooty ground of the asteroid. They climbed aboard the Captain's spaceship. "According to my calculations, we should be on our way."

“But we’re still parked here on the asteroid,” said Cathy.

“Of course we are. The entire asteroid, with us on it, is now on its way toward Earth.” Danny and Cathy exchanged startled looks. “That’s right. I, Captain Contraption have done it again, with your help, of course. We shall be the first to bring an asteroid back to Earth. What could be simpler?”

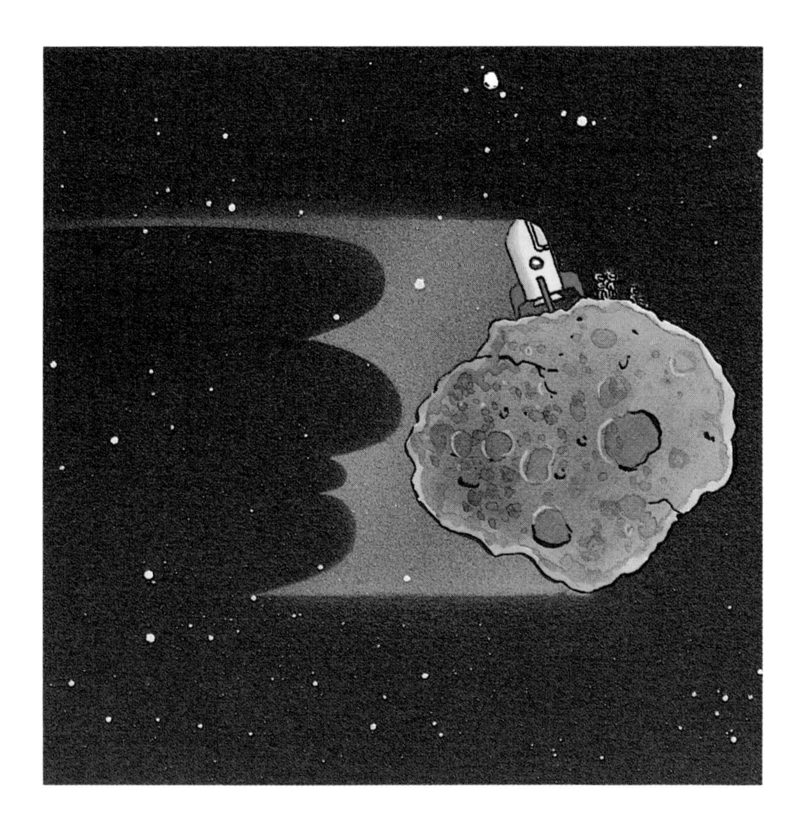

IN THE ASTEROID BELT

The Captain got out a simple chart of the **solar system**. "Here we are in the asteroid belt between Mars and Jupiter. Hundreds of billions of asteroids drift through the belt. Small ones, about a kilometer or a half mile across, are everywhere. A couple hundred asteroids are larger than 100 kilometers, or about 60 miles, across. At least a half dozen have been found that are over 300 kilometers, or about 200 miles, across. The largest is Ceres (SEAR-ez). It's over 1,000 kilometers in diameter!"

"I know about Ceres," said Cathy. "Ceres was the first asteroid discovered. An Italian astronomer named Piazzi discovered it in 1801. He thought he had discovered a new **planet**. Ceres is twice as large as any other asteroid. But it's not quite a planet. Soon after the discovery of Ceres, many more asteroids were found. Astronomers have now cataloged over 2,200 asteroids! But even so, if all the asteroids were put together, it would make an object that was still smaller than the moon."

"Someday I might come back for Ceres," said the Captain. "But for now, I thought I would start with one of the smaller ones."

"But why take an asteroid to Earth?" asked Cathy.

"Minerals!" shouted the Captain. "We'll all be rich!"

"But how will you get it to Earth without dropping it into the ocean or blasting a big hole in the ground?" asked Danny.

"We don't have to take it onto Earth," replied the Captain. "We just have to get it near Earth. We'll park it in Earth's orbit. There in space it could be mined to build space stations and spaceships. It would be another **satellite**. They could build right on it. They could use sunlight for power. They could build solar panels and factories and living quarters. Anytime they needed to add on, they could just melt a bit more of the asteroid. What could be simpler?"

"You know," said Cathy, "we didn't have to come all the way out here to get an asteroid."

"What do you mean?" asked the Captain. "Aren't all asteroids in the asteroid belt?"

"Most of the asteroids are in the belt but

not all," said Cathy. "A few groups of asteroids drift around the solar system. They all orbit the sun. But still, they're not quite planets."

"If they're not quite planets," asked Danny, "then what are they?"

"Asteroids are called the minor planets or **planetesimals**," said Cathy. "Asteroids are rocks in space. They never became part of a real planet like the other rocks that were around when the planets were forming. Scientists want to study asteroids. They believe asteroids are made of **matter** that hasn't changed since the time when the planets formed."

MANY GROUPS OF ASTEROIDS

Cathy unrolled a color chart she had made at school. "One group is called the Amor Asteroids. The Amor Asteroids are just like the ones here in the asteroid belt, except their **orbits** carry them closer to the sun than Mars. Most are about five to ten kilometers, or about three to six miles, across. But some are larger. My favorite is a funny-shaped one named Eros. It's skinny, but it's about 20 miles long. Scientists think it's a fragment from a crash between two asteroids."

"Then I didn't need to come all this way to get an asteroid," said Captain Contraption. "I could have found one without passing Mars!"

"You could have found one right near Earth," said Danny. "Look at Cathy's chart. It shows another group of asteroids. They're called the Apollo Asteroids. They're also called Earth crossing or Earth grazing asteroids because they cross Earth's orbit around the sun."

"And," added Cathy, "there is even a group of asteroids that orbit the sun closer than Earth! They're called Aten Asteroids."

"Well isn't that nice. I wish you two had told me about these other asteroids sooner. We could have saved ourselves a lot of trouble. Are there any other asteroids I should know about?"

"Yes," said Cathy. "There are two groups of asteroids that follow the same orbit as Jupiter. Each group is in a special place where the gravity of Jupiter and the sun are in balance. They are called the Trojan Asteroids. Astronomers gave them the names of the heroes of some old stories about the Trojan wars."

"Well it's too late now anyway," said the Captain. "We're on our way toward Earth... I think. So just relax and enjoy the ride."

CROSSING
APOLLO

THE FIRST UH-OH

The first "uh-oh" came a couple of weeks after Captain Contraption's rocket had started the asteroid moving.

"Captain Contraption," said Cathy. "This asteroid is turning around, right?"

"Just about everything in the solar system is turning," replied the Captain.

"And it has a day side and a night side, right?"

"Certainly it does," said the Captain. "Just about everything in the solar system has a day and a night side. What are you getting at?"

"Well, when you fired your big rocket, we were on the day side. So doesn't that mean we're traveling away from the sun?"

"Uh-oh," said Captain Contraption.

"What's wrong?" asked Danny.

"Now don't be alarmed," said Captain Contraption. He looked a bit sheepish. "But I think Cathy has a point. We should have fired the rocket when it was exactly midnight. That would have pushed the asteroid toward the sun."

"What should we do now?" asked Cathy.

"This asteroid is going who knows where," said the Captain. "Let's get out of here." They got into the Captain's spaceship and took off.

"Where are we going now?" asked Danny.

"We're off to outer space," said Captain Contraption. "This has all been planned. Really. We'll find another asteroid and start over."

They soon saw another asteroid. "There, you see. I told you we'd find another one." said the Captain.

"That's not too surprising," said Danny. "There are hundreds of billions of them out here in the asteroid belt."

"But this one is big," said Cathy. "It's not quite a planet, but it is big."

CAMPING OUT ON AN ASTEROID

They landed on the dark cratered surface. Danny and Cathy went exploring while the Captain got to work with rocket parts. Even on the day side of the asteroid it was fairly dark. They were far from the sun, so the light was not as bright as on Earth. The ground was very dark. The sky, of course, was deep black. It was a great place to look at stars.

"I thought we would be able to see more asteroids," said Danny, looking out at the stars. "I mean, aren't there supposed to be hundreds of billions of them?"

"I know what you mean," said Cathy. "I thought it would be like seeing boulders in the sky. But we can only see one or sometimes two other asteroids. They're so far away they look like faint stars."

While Cathy and Danny explored the asteroid, Captain Contraption experimented with some weird-looking machines. One drilled holes in the ground. The other sent chunks of rock into space. Some of his inventions shook apart and others exploded silently, for there was no air on the asteroid to carry the sounds from the fireworks. Captain Contraption told Cathy and Danny to make themselves at home. They would be there a few days.

Camping out on the asteroid was fun. Danny and Cathy hopped about on the tiny world. They leaped hundreds of meters over the ground and landed hundreds of meters away. Once, they hopped all the way around the asteroid. In the extremely low gravity, they could do great flips and fancy dives. After each dive, they settled back to the ground as softly as a feather falling through the thick air of Earth.

Cathy and Danny found lots of craters on the asteroid. Some were as small as a dime. Some were as large as a football stadium. They used a microscope and found craters as small as the head of a pin.

"**Micrometeorites**," said Cathy. "That's what made these tiny craters. It says in this book that the asteroids and the moon and everything in space are bombarded by tiny specks of dust. The specs are called micrometeorites. They sandblast everything. They travel through space at ten kilometers per second. That's about 20,000 miles per hour!"

"That must be why this asteroid looks so worn down," said Danny. "Nothing has sharp edges except our footprints."

"It's a good thing we have tough space suits or those micrometeorites would make us look worn down, too!"

Once Danny threw a rock at a low angle. About an hour later, the rock came sailing by. It just barely missed them. Every hour or so they had to watch out for the asteroid's new satellite. That gave them a great idea for a practical joke. They made a pie with a plate and the Captain's shaving cream. Then they threw it. Sure enough, about an hour later it appeared over the horizon and whizzed by them. They marked the spot where it came by. When the little satellite was due to come again, they called the Captain. "Stand right here and close your eyes," they told him.

Soon the pie appeared low over the asteroid. When the pie was about 10 meters away, they yelled for him to open his eyes. The surprised Captain managed to duck just in time and the pie streaked on by. Now there were two objects they had to watch out for. Each hour the tiny satellites, a rock and a pie, whizzed by. A few days later, the Captain got careless and the orbiting pie splattered him squarely in the face.

LOOKING FOR THE RIGHT ASTEROID

The Captain finally decided that the asteroid they were on was too large to move. They set off in the spaceship to find a better one.

"Look," said Captain Contraption. He pointed toward a huge asteroid. "I, Captain Contraption, and my two able assistants have found an asteroid with a moon! We'll all be famous!"

"It's Pallas!" Cathy shouted. "My favorite asteroid! It already is famous. It was the second one discovered. It was found in 1802, the year after Ceres was discovered. But only recently astronomers learned that it had a tiny moon."

"Oh," said the Captain."Well, we can at least be the first to explore it."

Danny, Cathy, and the Captain spent a day exploring Pallas. Then they visited its tiny moon. When they stood on the moon and looked up,

Pallas took up most of the sky. It was an amazing and beautiful sight. It was also just a bit scary to see that huge asteroid so close overhead.

Cathy and Danny wouldn't let the Captain take Pallas or its moon, so they left. The Captain headed the spaceship away from the sun.

"Where are we going," asked Danny.

"You'll see," said the Captain. "This has all been planned." For weeks they saw no asteroids. They were beyond the asteroid belt now. Then they finally saw a tiny dot before them.

As it grew closer, Danny said, "It looks like a dumbbell."

"I think it looks like two eggs stuck together," said Cathy.

"Look," said Captain Contraption as they drew near the strange asteroid. "We have discovered a double asteroid! We'll all be famous!"

"It's Hektor!" shouted Cathy. "My favorite asteroid! It already is famous. Hektor is the largest Trojan asteroid."

"Oh," said the Captain." Well we can at least be the first to explore it."

"I thought you said Eros was your favorite," said Danny.

"Eros is my favorite Amor asteroid," explained Cathy. "Pallas is my favorite regular asteroid because it has the little moon. And

Hektor is my favorite Trojan asteroid because it is so unusual."

"Don't you have a favorite Apollo asteroid?" asked Danny.

"I don't like the Apollo Asteroids. They might crash into Earth some time and that would be terrible."

After landing, Danny and Cathy headed off to explore the strange twin world. As they crossed the surface, the opposite part of the asteroid rose over the horizon. It grew and grew until it took up most of the sky. "Let's cross over," cried Cathy. Together they leaped into space. They arrived a half hour later at the other part of the asteroid. It was too dark to tell whether the two parts of the asteroid were touching. Danny and Cathy spent the rest of their time on Hektor jumping back and forth between the two great lobes of the asteroid.

Back aboard the ship, Danny was very quiet. "What's the matter, Danny?" asked Cathy.

"I was just thinking," said Danny. "I wonder what will happen to the first asteroid we landed on."

"I think the Captain sent it out of the asteroid belt," said Cathy. "It will probably drift in space in an odd orbit around the sun."

"But what if it goes in toward the sun and Earth?"

"The Captain's rocket pushed it out away from the sun," Cathy reassured him.

"But the gravity of Jupiter could swing it around and head it back toward Earth," Danny said. "What if it hits the Earth?"

"Oh come now," interrupted the Captain. "Asteroids are always running into the Earth, I'm told. Not to worry."

"It's true that **meteoroids** run into the Earth every day," said Cathy. "But it's rare for a big asteroid to hit Earth. That only happens about once in a million years."

"What would happen if it did?" asked Danny.

"It could be really bad. Even a small asteroid would do a lot of damage. Tens of thousands of years ago, an asteroid about 100 meters in diameter crashed into Earth in what is now Arizona. It made a **crater** about a kilometer, or about a half mile, across and a couple hundred meters deep! Everything for a hundred kilometers around was killed."

"It wasn't me," said the Captain. "I wasn't around then."

"You know that millions of years ago the dinosaurs suddenly became extinct," Cathy continued. "Some scientists believe a large asteroid may have crashed into the Earth. They think that the dust from such a crash could have blocked out the sunlight. That would make plants die and turn everything cold. That may have made the dinosaurs disappear."

WHAT'S THE DIFFERENCE?

"**Meteor**, meteoroid, **meteorite**... they all sound the same. What's the difference between them?" asked Danny.

"That's easy," said Cathy. "A meteor is what you see in the sky as a shooting star. It's that glowing streak that happens when a rock from space runs into Earth's atmosphere going 20,000 miles per hour. The rock rubs against the air molecules and heats up until it glows. On any dark night, you can see about six meteors each hour.

"When the rock is in space it's called a meteoroid. A meteoroid could be smaller than a grain of sand or as big as a car. If the meteoroid is big, it lights up the sky with a spectacular fireball. It lasts for several seconds.

"If the piece of rock from space reaches the ground, then it's called a meteorite. Not many of them make it to the ground though," explained Cathy. "Most are small — sand grain to popcorn sized. They burn up from the friction with the air.

But every day several tons of meteorites fall on the Earth."

"Tons! Did you say *tons* every day?" asked the Captain.

"That's right," Cathy said. "Most of it is in the form of dust, called micrometeorites, and the fine soot from the meteors that burn up when they hit the Earth's atmosphere. Only a few large meteorites land on Earth. The largest meteorite on display is about the size of a car and weighs over 34 tons!"

"But where do the meteors and meteorites come from?" asked Danny.

"Astronomers believe that the rocks in space, the meteoroids, are the rocks that were left over when the planets formed. It's the stuff that never became planets. That's why scientists on Earth want to study meteorites. They can learn about rocks that haven't changed since the time when planets formed."

"So meteoroids are just like asteroids," said Danny. "But what are they made of?"

"Some of the meteorites are made of iron and nickel and are very heavy. Some are stony and look more like earth rocks. Most meteoroids are made of the same materials as asteroids. They're probably pieces of asteroids that crashed together and broke apart."

"There, you see," said the Captain, "iron and nickel — minerals. What did I tell you? We could have all been rich."

"And some meteoroids," Cathy continued, "may be dust and rocks from comets."

"**Comets**!" exclaimed Captain Contraption. "Did you say comets? Those majestic and graceful things with the great long **tails**?"

COMETS

"That's right, Captain," said Cathy. "Those comet tails are very dusty. A comet leaves behind lots of dust and little rocks as it travels through space. When Earth passes through the dusty path left by a comet, the dust burns up in the atmosphere creating a **meteor shower**. There are several meteor showers that happen on the same date every year as Earth passes through a part of space where a comet has been. One of the best meteor showers happens in the middle of August, every year. During this shower, up to one meteor every minute can be seen from Earth."

Captain Contraption grew interested. "Besides the dust, what are comets made of?"

"Comets are big dirty snowballs in space," said Danny.

"You mean comets are made of ice?" asked the Captain, suddenly excited.

"Right," said Danny. "Some of the ice is frozen water. Some of it is frozen gases, like

methane and carbon dioxide. People call frozen carbon dioxide dry ice."

"And how big did you say these comets were?" asked the Captain. He had a sly look on his face.

"Anywhere from one to 50 kilometers, or about a half mile to 30 miles across."

"Hmmm, not bad," smiled the Captain. "And where might we find comets?"

"I'm not sure," said Danny. "Let me look in my astronomy book. Oh, here it is. It says that comets, hundreds of billions of them, may be found in a vast cloud which surrounds the sun. It's named Oort's Cloud after Jan Oort."

Captain Contraption frowned. "So this guy Jan Oort owns the comets?"

"Oh no," said Danny. "He was a Dutch astronomer. In 1950, he studied the orbits of comets. He figured out that the comets must be coming from this faraway cloud. Nobody has ever seen the cloud. They just think it must be out there. Scientists want to study comets. They think the Oort Cloud was probably left behind from the cloud of matter that formed the sun and planets and everything else in the solar system. Scientists think the stuff that comets are made of has stayed the same since the solar system formed about five billion years ago!"

"Great!" shouted the Captain, growing excited. "What do you say we head on over to Oort's Cloud and pick up a few comets. Ah, exactly where is Oort's Cloud."

"It's pretty far away, Captain Contraption. How long would it take us to get to Pluto?"

"Pluto, Pluto, Pluto, let me see." Captain Contraption took out a calculator. He set it on the console and began counting on his fingers. "From Earth, let's see, with full rocket power and a little gravity assist from Jupiter and Saturn, say I can get up to about 100,000 kilometers per hour. At that speed, I can make it to Pluto in about 12 years. From here on Hektor, about 10. Why do you ask?"

"Well, it says here that the Oort Cloud is about a thousand times farther away from Earth than Pluto. Since it would take us ten years to get to Pluto, it would take us about ten thousand years to get to the Oort Cloud!"

"That may be a problem," replied the Captain, raising one eyebrow.

"But we don't have to go all the way out there to get a comet," said Danny.

"We don't?" asked the Captain.

"Sometimes comets are bumped out of the Oort Cloud by the gravity of a passing star. Some of these comets fall in toward the sun. It takes them tens of thousands of years to get to the inner solar system."

"Hmmm." said the Captain. "I don't know if I can wait that long."

"You won't have to wait," said Danny. "Comets fall in toward the sun from the Oort Cloud all the time. Some comets have long narrow orbits and travel far outside the orbits of the planets. The ones that take more than 200 years to complete their orbit around the sun are called long period comets. They go around the sun like the Earth. But they're not quite planets.

"Some long period comets get bumped out of their paths around the sun by the gravity of a planet. Some may be thrown out of the solar system. Others may slow down and fall into a smaller orbit around the sun. Comets that orbit the sun in less than 200 years are called short period comets. One named Comet Enke orbits the sun in only a bit over three years. The most famous comet, Comet Halley, takes about 75 years."

"That's still a long time to wait," said the Captain, disappointed.

"But they are already here," insisted Danny. "On any night there are about a dozen comets in the sky. Most are too faint to be seen from Earth except with large telescopes."

"A <u>dozen</u>, you say," said the Captain. "Danny, Cathy, we are now in the comet hunting business. I'll need your help. Let's set up on the dark side of an asteroid and get to work. You know, if we discover a comet, it will be named after us. We'll all be famous."

LOOKING FOR A COMET

So the three set up a comet patrol on the dark side of one of the Trojan asteroids that shared Jupiter's orbit. They spent long hours laying on their backs, carefully scanning the starry sky through large binoculars.

At first, they saw faint fuzzy objects they thought were comets. But they were only distant galaxies or faraway glowing clouds of gas and dust called nebulae (NEB-u-lee). After a while, the three comet hunters learned where these objects were among the stars. Then they stopped mistaking them for comets. One night Danny spotted something. "Hey, what's that?" he said. They all turned their binoculars to where Danny pointed. They saw an object. They watched it for a few hours. They could see that it moved against the background stars.

"This might be it," said the Captain. "Everybody to the ship."

They finally caught up to the strange

object. "It looks like a giant peanut," said Cathy. "Maybe it's another asteroid. Are you sure it's a comet? It doesn't have a tail."

"This far from the sun it wouldn't have one," explained Danny. "We're looking at the nucleus of the comet. When it gets closer to the sun, the heat from the sun will evaporate the ice. A big ball of gas, called the **coma**, will form around the nucleus. Then, sunlight and a stream of particles which flows out from the sun, called the **solar wind**, will push some of the gas and dust away from the coma. That will form the tail. That's why the tail always points away from the sun."

"Are we going to follow it?" asked Danny.

"My dear boy," said the Captain, "we're going to land on it!"

From a distance, the peanut-shaped object looked like an asteroid. But as they drew nearer, they saw that it had no craters, like the asteroids.

"This one looks like it's about eight or ten kilometers long," said Captain Contraption. He set the spaceship down gently on the day side of the strange little world.

"I thought comets were supposed to be made of ice," said Cathy. "This all looks dark, like the dirt on the asteroids."

"Just keep watching," replied Danny. "The ice is underneath. It's covered with a layer of dust. Just keep watching."

A STRANGE JOURNEY

The comet journeyed past the asteroid belt and on toward Mars. A thin mist appeared above the ground. Cathy and Danny explored the comet. They found many tiny geysers of gas erupting in cracks in the dark dust. Strange little eruptions startled Captain Contraption as he assembled his usual maze of pipes. He was lifted off his feet when a large burst of gas shot up right beneath him.

"As we near the sun," Danny told them, "the ice changes from a solid to a gas. Then the gas erupts through the dust. Some of the rocks and soil will be carried away. That will happen more and more as we near the sun."

"Don't worry," said the Captain, "we'll be getting off soon. Just as soon as I finish my newest invention." The invention was another mess of tubes and metal balls topped by a huge upside-down rocket engine. Cathy and Danny were a bit concerned.

The comet swept inside the orbit of Mars. More and more streamers of gas broke through the dark crust. They could see patches of light-colored ice now. The comet had a foggy appearance. Soon they could no longer see stars. "Don't worry," said the Captain, "I'm almost done." Danny and Cathy explored the fantastic landscape that changed every day.

The comet rotated as it traveled through space. A full cycle of light and dark was about ten hours long. During the five-hour daytime when they faced the sun, the geysers shot skyward. As they turned away from the sun for a five-hour night, they could see glowing streamers flowing off toward the tail.

As the comet moved between Mars and Earth, the Captain made an announcement.

"As usual, I have amazed even myself. I will now start my invention. If my calculations are correct, we should be able to capture this comet and take it to the moon. The moon, as you know, has no water. Water is vital to people who live on the moon. A comet is a huge, dirty iceberg. All we need to do is take this comet to the moon. What could be simpler? We'll all be rich!"

"But we're traveling at 60,000 miles per hour!" Danny said. "How will you get the comet onto the moon without blasting a big hole in the ground?"

"We don't have to take it onto the moon," replied Captain Contraption. "We just have to get it near the moon. We'll park it in orbit around the moon. Then it can be mined in space for water. What could be simpler?"

"But if it's that close to the sun, won't the sun evaporate it?" asked Cathy.

"Details, details, details," said Captain Contraption. "I'll let you two worry about the details. Now everybody step back." The Captain counted down. A huge flame flared skyward. The ground shook. Heat from the rocket engine made the comet's ices erupt all around them. The engine was lost in a thick fog. As usual, it exploded. They all fell to the ground. Out of the mist came the usual confetti of rocket engine fragments. Captain Contraption got to his feet again with a satisfied smile. "Perfect," he said, looking at the large crater where the rocket had been. "Let's get out of here." Cathy and Danny agreed.

The second "uh-oh" occurred as they were preparing to take off in the Captain's spaceship.

THE SECOND UH-OH.

"Uh-oh," said the Captain.

"What's wrong?" asked Cathy and Danny.

"Our spaceship won't start."

And so there they were, stranded on a comet, hurtling toward the sun. From inside the ship they watched the ground around them disappear. The Captain worked on the ship. A vast cloud of gas and dust formed around the comet and grew.

"What happens to comets when they get close to the sun?" asked Cathy. "Does it melt all the ice?"

"The sun turns some of the ice into gas each time the comet goes by," said Danny. "Eventually, after a comet has gone around the sun many times, all the ice may disappear. That may leave behind a rocky core of dirt, dust, and rocks."

"Then it would be just like an asteroid," said Cathy.

The dark ground was mostly gone now. Only a few scattered patches of rocks were left. Each day, several inches of the surface of the comet disappeared into space. Some rocks stayed behind, perched on pillars of ice that had been shaded from the warmth of the sun. The exposed ices evaporated. They left behind a landscape of weird ice towers and statues. Great cracks split the comet. One leg of the ship fell into a hole. It had formed when the ices vanished into space. Nearby a geyser shot clouds of gas and dust into space. On the day side of the comet, the sun grew larger each day.

"I have an announcement," said Danny. He was trying to cheer everyone up. "We are the only inhabitants of the largest object in the solar system. The coma of this comet is bigger than Jupiter, and the tail probably extends back as far as Mars."

"And yet," sighed the Captain, "it's still not quite a planet, is it?"

"Nope," said Danny. "The nucleus is small. And there isn't much substance to the coma and the tail of a comet. All the matter in the tail could fit in a little kid's wagon."

At last the comet swung around the sun and headed back out into space. Each day the geysers got smaller. The evaporation slowed. The surface fog thinned enough so that they could again see the landscape of the comet. The streamers of gas coming from cracks and holes weakened and disappeared. Soon they noticed that the ice on the comet's surface was getting dirty again. Dust began to fall back from space. It covered the ground and their spacecraft.

Danny and Cathy went out exploring. They tried to build a snow sculpture, but the ices were too dry. They wouldn't stick together. Captain Contraption made a sled out of some tubing. They took turns pulling each other over the comet. He improved it one day with a small rocket and some flashing lights for night sledding. Danny and Cathy wanted him to try it out first. The Captain raced across the comet on the rocket sled and went over a small rise. The sled flew off the comet and headed for space. Captain Contraption fell off. In the low gravity, it took him about an hour to fall to the ground. They never saw the sled again.

RESCUED!

The streamers stopped and the fog disappeared. They could again see the stars. Then one night, they saw an object moving across the sky. At first they thought it might be an asteroid. Soon they could see that it was a freight rocket. It was headed directly for the comet. Captain Contraption rigged some lights. They were soon rescued.

"That's right," the skipper of the freighter told them when they were safely aboard. "We saw that wild signal you sent up the other day. It looked like a sled with a bunch of lights on it. So we came right over. Quite clever, Captain Contraption. But how did you know we were out here?"

The Captain never answered the skipper's question. Instead, he winked at Danny and Cathy. "This has all been planned," he said.

"We'll write a book about our adventures," he told them as they headed toward Earth. "We'll call it, Marooned on a Comet."

Cathy and Danny rolled their eyes and laughed. "What could be simpler?" they shouted together. "We'll all be rich!"

GLOSSARY

Asteroid: A small planet or planetesimal (miniature planet) in orbit around the sun. Asteroids come in different shapes and sizes.

Asteroid Belt: A region of space between the orbits of Mars and Jupiter that contains most of the asteroids.

Coma: A cloud of gas that forms around the nucleus of a comet as it nears the sun. Also called the head. The coma can grow to be 100,000 kilometers (about 60,000 miles) in diameter.

Comet: A solid object made mostly of ices. As a comet nears the sun, the ices change into gas. Gas and dust from the comet form a huge head or coma and a tail extending millions of kilometers into space.

Crater: A bowl shaped cavity. Craters are caused by the impact of a meteorite, micrometeorite, asteroid, or some object.

Gravity: A property that causes things to attract and be attracted by all other things. Gravity causes matter to clump together.

Matter: The substance things are made of. Matter is anything that takes up space and has weight. It can be a gas, liquid, or solid.

Meteor: A glowing streak of light caused by the heating of a piece of rock or dust from space as it collides with Earth's atmosphere. Also called "shooting stars."

Meteor Shower: A shower of meteors caused when Earth's atmosphere and swarms of dust and rocks in space collide.

Meteorite: A meteor particle that reaches the surface of Earth or another body in the solar system.

Meteoroid: A rock floating in space.

Micrometeorite: A tiny particle of dust slowed down by Earth's atmosphere so that it floats to the surface of Earth. Also, micrometeorites are tiny particles traveling through the solar system at high speed. They hit planets, moons, asteroids, spacecraft, and other objects.

Orbit: The curved path of a planet, satellite, or other object around another object.

Planet: A body moving in orbit around a star. There are nine known planets in our solar system: Mercury, Venus, Earth, Mars, Jupiter, Saturn, Uranus, Neptune, and Pluto. There are also thousands of minor planets or asteroids.

Planetesimals: Also called minor planets. They are asteroids, rocks that never became part of a true planet.

Satellite: Any object that is in orbit around another object. A satellite may be natural, such as a moon, or artificial, such as an orbiting weather satellite.

Solar System: The family of objects that surrounds the sun, including planets, moons, asteroids, and comets.

Solar Wind: A stream of high speed particles (pieces of atoms) flowing out from the sun through the solar system.

Tail: The part of a comet that streams out away from the coma, made of gas and dust.